THE MAN IN THE IRON MASK

Vol. 1: The Three Musketeers

Adapted from the novel by ALEXANDRE DUMAS

Writer
Roy Thomas
Special Thanks to Deborah Sherer & Freeman Henry

Penciler
Hugo Petrus

Inker
Tom Palmer

Letterer
Virtual Calligraphy's Joe Caramagna

Colorist
June Chung

Cover
Marko Djurdjevic

Special Thanks to Chris Allo

Associate Editor
Nicole Boose

Editor
Ralph Macchio

Editor in Chief
Joe Quesada

Publisher
Dan Buckley

Spotlight

MARVEL®

VISIT US AT
www.abdopublishing.com

Reinforced library bound edition published in 2009 by Spotlight, a division of the ABDO Group, 8000 West 78th Street, Edina, Minnesota 55439. Spotlight produces high-quality reinforced library bound editions for schools and libraries. Published by agreement with Marvel Characters, Inc.

Library of Congress Cataloging-in-Publication Data

Thomas, Roy, 1940-
  The man in the iron mask / adapted from the novel by Alexandre Dumas ; Roy Thomas, writer ; Hugo Petrus, penciler ; Tom Palmer, inker ; Virtual Calligraphy's Joe Caramagna, letterer ; June Chung, colorist. -- Reinforced library bound ed.
     v. cm.
  "Marvel."
  Contents: v. 1. The three musketeers -- v. 2. High treason -- v. 3. The iron mask -- v. 4. The man in the iron mask -- v. 5. The death of a titan -- v. 6. Musketeers no more.
  ISBN 9781599615943 (v. 1) -- ISBN 9781599615950 (v. 2) -- ISBN 9781599615967 (v. 3) -- ISBN 9781599615974 (v. 4) -- ISBN 9781599615981 (v. 5) -- ISBN 9781599615998 (v. 6)
  Summary: Retells, in comic book format, Alexandre Dumas' tale of political intrigue, romance, and adventure in seventeenth-century France.
  [1. Dumas, Alexandre, 1802-1870.--Adaptations. 2. Graphic novels. 3. Adventure and adventurers--Fiction. 4. France--History--Louis XIII, 1610-1643--Fiction.] I. Dumas, Alexandre, 1802-1870. II. Petrus, Hugo. VI. Title.
PZ7.7.T518 Man 2009
[Fic]--dc22   2008035321

All Spotlight books have reinforced library bindings and
are manufactured in the United States of America.

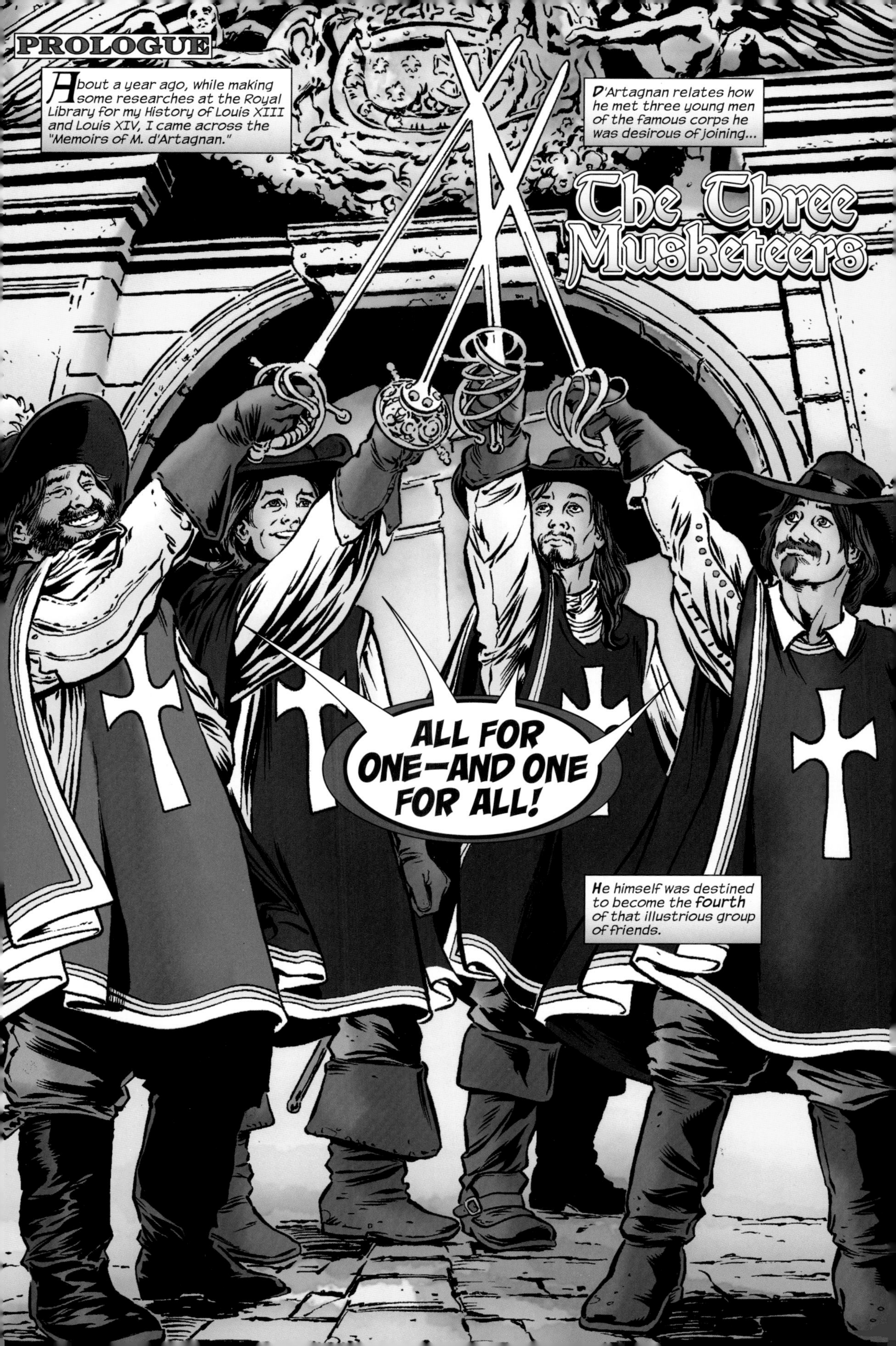
PROLOGUE
About a year ago, while making some researches at the Royal Library for my History of Louis XIII and Louis XIV, I came across the "Memoirs of M. d'Artagnan."
D'Artagnan relates how he met three young men of the famous corps he was desirous of joining...
The Three Musketeers
ALL FOR ONE—AND ONE FOR ALL!
He himself was destined to become the fourth of that illustrious group of friends.

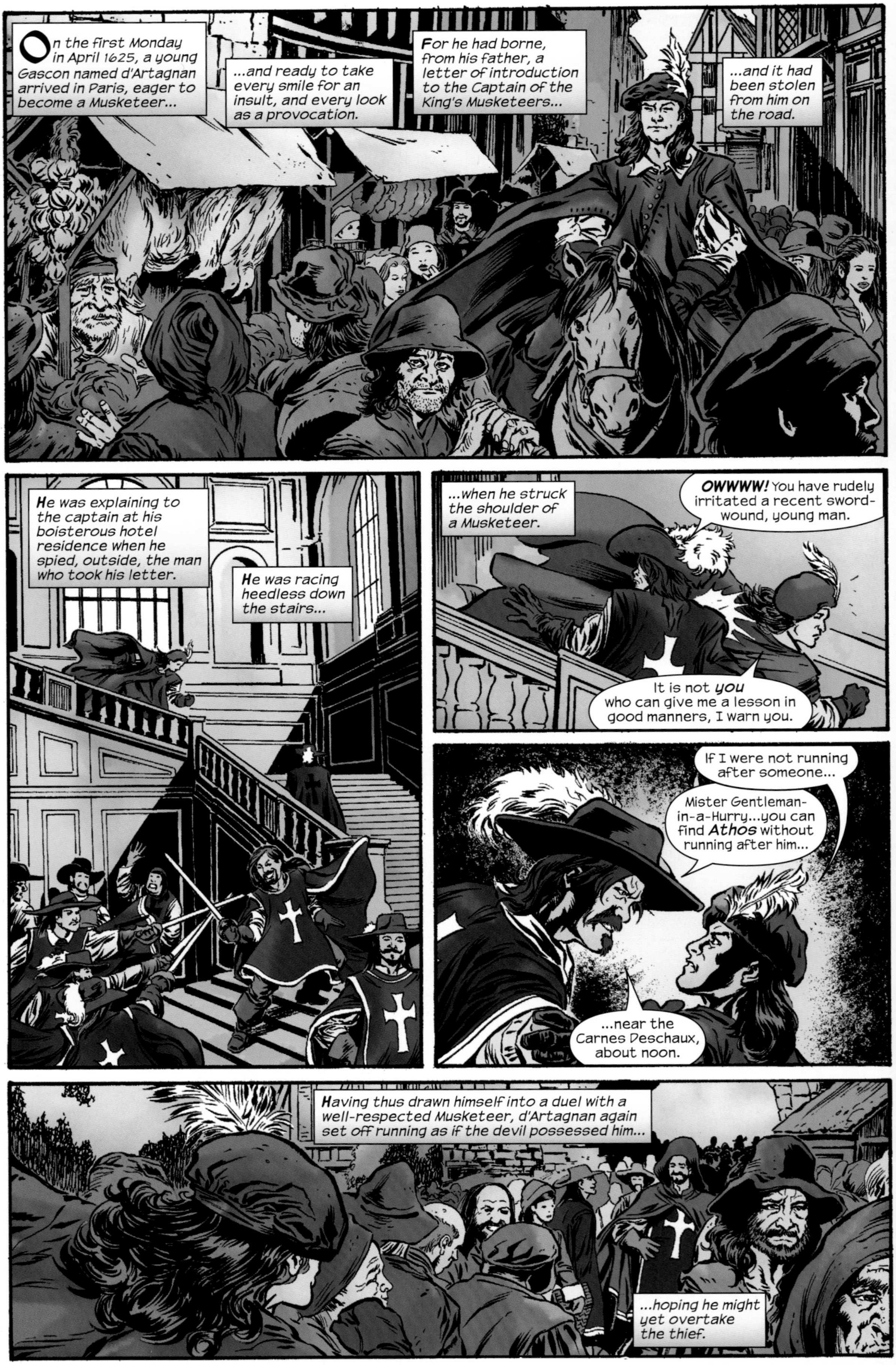
On the first Monday in April 1625, a young Gascon named d'Artagnan arrived in Paris, eager to become a Musketeer...
...and ready to take every smile for an insult, and every look as a provocation.
For he had borne, from his father, a letter of introduction to the Captain of the King's Musketeers...
...and it had been stolen from him on the road.
He was explaining to the captain at his boisterous hotel residence when he spied, outside, the man who took his letter.
He was racing heedless down the stairs...
...when he struck the shoulder of a Musketeer.
OWWWW! You have rudely irritated a recent sword-wound, young man.
It is not you who can give me a lesson in good manners, I warn you.
If I were not running after someone...
Mister Gentleman-in-a-Hurry...you can find Athos without running after him...
...near the Carnes Deschaux, about noon.
Having thus drawn himself into a duel with a well-respected Musketeer, d'Artagnan again set off running as if the devil possessed him...
...hoping he might yet overtake the thief.

But as he raced between two men talking, the wind blew out the giant one's cape...

Vertubleu! You must be mad!

You must be chastised for running against *Porthos* in this fashion--

--at one o'clock, behind the Luxembourg Garden.

Ahead, d'Artagnan recognized *Aramis* talking to three of the King's guards...

...and resolved to be polite to this third of the trio of famed Musketeers.

I believe, Monsieur Aramis...

...that you stand upon...

...a handkerchief you would be sorry to lose?

You are deceived, sir. This handkerchief is not mine.

But-- I saw--

HAH HAH!

Will you persist in saying, most discreet Aramis, that you are not on good terms with Madame de Bois-Tracy--

--when that gracious lady has the kindness to lend you her handkerchief?

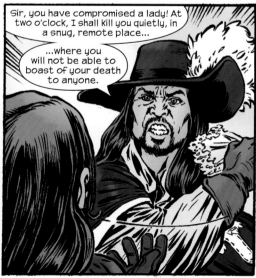

Sir, you have compromised a lady! At two o'clock, I shall kill you quietly, in a snug, remote place...

...where you will not be able to boast of your death to anyone.

Duels at twelve...and one...and two...with three men, each of whom is capable of killing three d'Artagnans.

At least, if I am killed, I shall be killed by a Musketeer!

*Being acquainted with no one in Paris, d'Artagnan went to his appointment with Athos without a second...but Athos had **two** such...*

I, humble d'Artagnan, offer you my excuses, gentlemen...

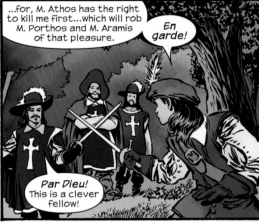

...for, M. Athos has the right to kill me first...which will rob M. Porthos and M. Aramis of that pleasure.

En garde!

Par Dieu! This is a clever fellow!

Fighting here, are you, Musketeers--in the shadow of the monastery, in defiance of the edicts?

It was five of the Guards who served Cardinal Richelieu...the Churchman who rivaled in power even Louis XIII himself.

*If the King had **his** Musketeers, the Cardinal must have his Guards...and the swordsmen were rivals, even as their masters were.*

Gentlemen... sheathe your swords, and follow me--or we will charge upon you!

There are five of them... and we are but three. Yet...

Gentlemen... it appears to me we are **four.**

Well, then! Athos, Porthos, Aramis, and d'Artagnan--

Forward!

And the nine combatants rushed upon each other with a fury that did not exclude a certain degree of method.

Soon, one of the Cardinal's Guards was dead...the others were wounded and fled.

And d'Artagnan's heart swam in delight to be at least an *apprentice* Musketeer.

Later, after a mission involving the Queen, the Duke of Buckingham, and the woman known as "Milady," d'Artagnan was finally offered a commission in the Musketeers.

In time, Athos returned to his estate...Porthos wed a rich widow...Aramis became a monk...and d'Artagnan, a famous soldier.

Twenty years after...

...the four friends united once more, to undertake a mission vital to France.

Their foe on that occasion was the son of "Milady"--he who wore the face of Evil.

More years passed.

By the time the young Louis XIV became King, only d'Artagnan remained a Musketeer, now Captain of the force he once dreamed of joining.

Athos had a noble son...the Viscount Bragelonne, whose name was...

Raoul...

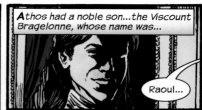

You must cease torturing yourself.

How could I, father...

...when I must watch from a distance as the *woman I love*--the beautiful Louise de la Valliere--has become the mistress of our new young King?

He stole her affections...while I was on a mission for the crown!

I shall speak with the King...for he knows I have wished to contract marriage between yourself and the lady.

But the audience between King and aristocrat did not go well...

Do you hesitate to grant my request, sire?

I do not hesitate. I *refuse.*

I *love* Louise de la Valliere.

Then Athos drew his sword...and broke it across his knee.

Son of Louis XIII, you begin your reign badly--by abduction and disloyalty!

You are now become our enemy, sire.

The King sent d'Artagnan to arrest Athos...

I am ordered to escort you to prison.

I am quite ready to go with you.

As the pair reached the Bastille, they were surprised to see an old friend emerging from a carriage...

...Aramis, now known also as M. d'Herblay, who had become the Bishop of Vannes.

My old friends!

To spare Athos embarrassment, d'Artagnan convinced the governor of the dreaded Bastille--their old Musketeer comrade M. Baisemeaux--that he had invited them, as well as Aramis, for dinner.

During the meal, d'Artagnan found an excuse to slip away, to try to convince the King to rescind his arrest order...

Our Captain of Musketeers swore he would return in time for dessert...

...and I see he has kept his word!

Alas, however, Athos and I must take our leave.

The King has set you at liberty, my friend.

My thanks, for persuading him to do so--but I can only return to my chateau... my solitude...

...and my son's despair.

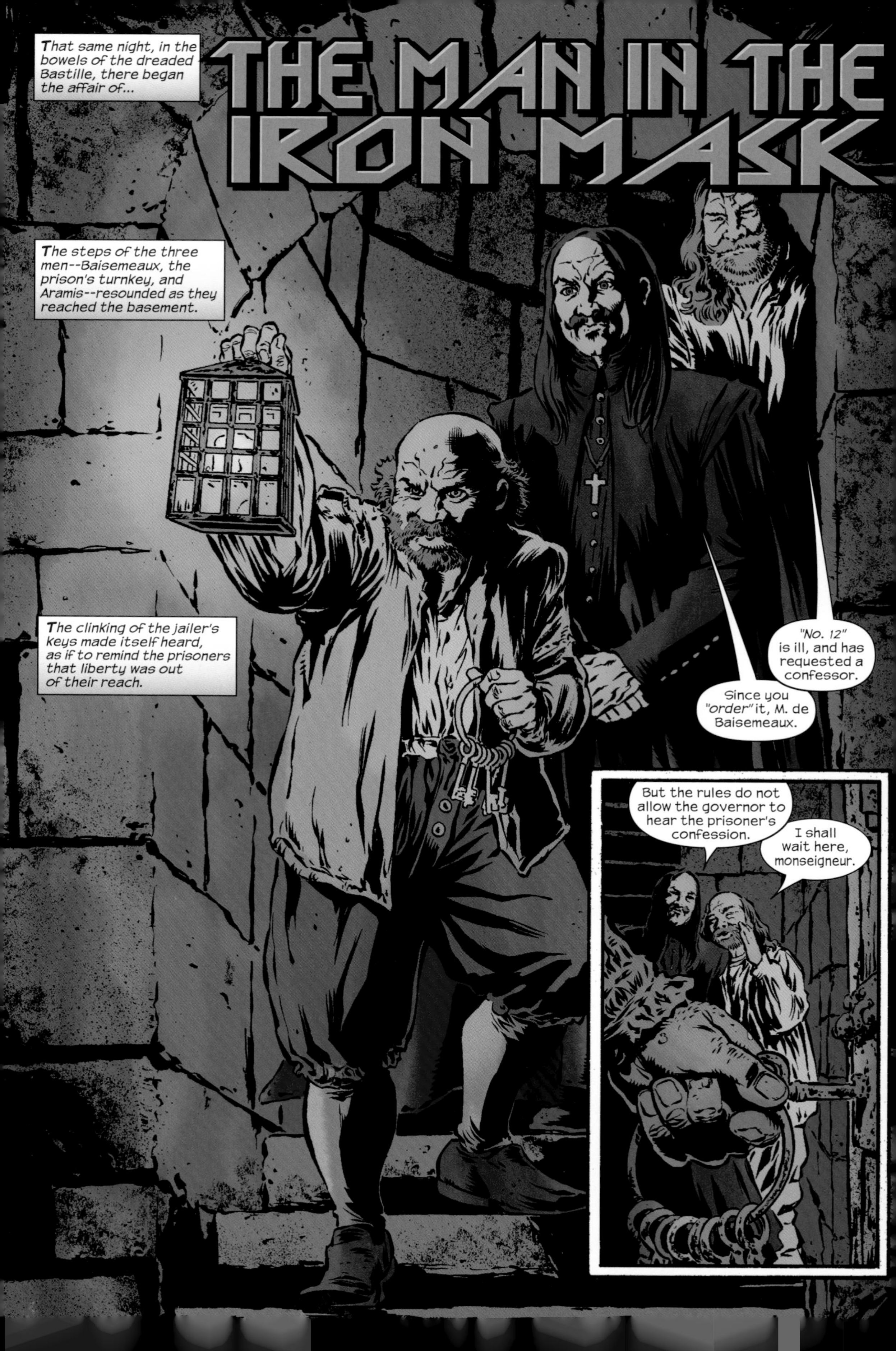
That same night, in the bowels of the dreaded Bastille, there began the affair of...
THE MAN IN THE IRON MASK
The steps of the three men--Baisemeaux, the prison's turnkey, and Aramis--resounded as they reached the basement.
The clinking of the jailer's keys made itself heard, as if to remind the prisoners that liberty was out of their reach.
"No. 12" is ill, and has requested a confessor.
Since you "order" it, M. de Baisemeaux.
But the rules do not allow the governor to hear the prisoner's confession.
I shall wait here, monseigneur.

Why are you here? Have you not desired a confessor?

Yes.

I thank you for coming.

But I am better...

...and thus I have no longer need of a confessor.

I have seen you before.

Perhaps. And you have nothing, then, to regret?

No.

Not even your liberty?

What do you call liberty, monsieur?

I call liberty the flowers, the air, light, the stars...

...the happiness of going whithersoever the nervous limbs of twenty years of age may wish to carry you.

If flowers constitute liberty, then I am free...

For, I have two roses, gathered yesterday evening from the governor's garden.

With every opening petal, they fill my chamber with a fragrance that embraces it.

When I stand on my chair, the air caresses my face through the bars of my window.

For light, I have the sun, a friend who visits me every day.

As to the stars...I could see them before you entered with your candle.

To return to our starting point...I am your confessor.

First tell me what *crime* I have committed...for, as my conscience does not accuse me, I aver that I am not a criminal.

We are often criminals in the sight of the great of the earth, not for having ourselves committed crimes...

...but because we know that crimes have been committed.

Yes...it is very possible that, in that light, I am a criminal.

And so you desired a confessor...

...after the note you found in your bread bade you ask for one.

If the King were to know of my presence here, I would tomorrow see glitter the executioner's axe...

...or the bottom of a dungeon more gloomy and more obscure than yours.

Since, then, we both wear masks, either let us both retain them... or put them aside together.

Tell me what you remember of your infancy...your childhood.

Perhaps it was then that your crime was committed.

First, I have a right to know--who *are* you?

Do you remember seeing, fifteen or eighteen years ago, in the village of Noisy-le-Sec, where your early years were spent...

"...a cavalier, accompanied by a lady in black silk, with flame-colored ribbons in her hair?"

"Yes. They told me he was the Abbé d'Herblay... who was also one of Louis XIII's Musketeers."

"Well, that Musketeer and Abbé, afterwards Bishop of Vannes, is your confessor now."

"I knew it. I recognized you..."

"...I was then called Philippe, and lived in a house and garden surrounded with walls whose boundaries I never left...

"...attended only by my tutor and my nurse, Perronnette.

"They were kind to me, but used to tell me that my father and mother were dead.

"Then, one day, eight years ago, I heard him cry out to her...

What is the matter?

The *letter!* A chance puff of air carried it from my desk--and it disappeared down the well--

--our last letter from the *Queen!*

You know she burns her letters every time she comes.

She will never believe that it was lost in this manner--and Mazarin will--

Well, 'tis no use hesitating...

Somebody must go down in the well and retrieve it--

--some villager who cannot read!

Yes! I will obtain a ladder long enough to reach down--

--while you find some stout-hearted youth.

"As soon as they were gone, I ran to the well.

"Something white and luminous glistened in the ripples of the water.

"The well seemed to draw me in with its large mouth and icy breath.

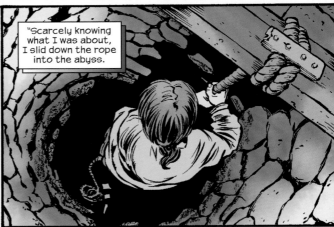

"Scarcely knowing what I was about, I slid down the rope into the abyss.

"I seized the dear letter...

"...which, alas, came in two in my grasp.

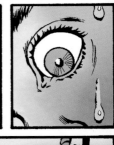

"I managed to retrieve the other half, as well, while becoming drenched...

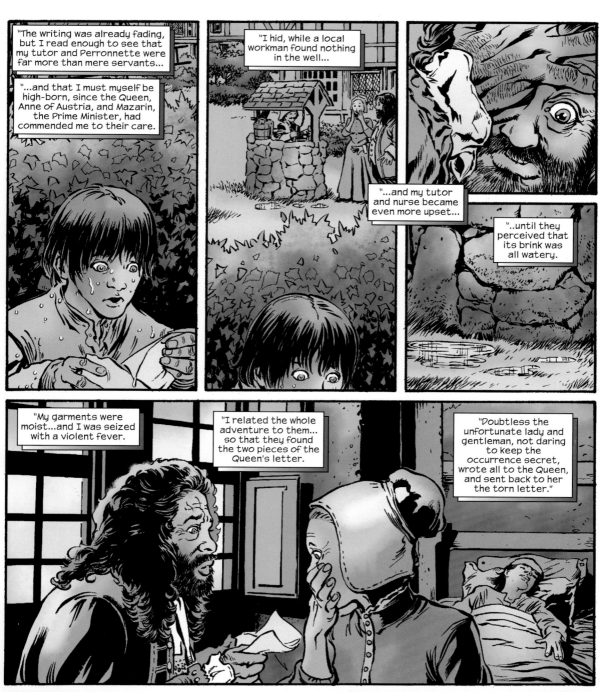

"The writing was already fading, but I read enough to see that my tutor and Perronnette were far more than mere servants...

"...and that I must myself be high-born, since the Queen, Anne of Austria, and Mazarin, the Prime Minister, had commended me to their care.

"I hid, while a local workman found nothing in the well...

"...and my tutor and nurse became even more upset...

"..until they perceived that its brink was all watery.

"My garments were moist...and I was seized with a violent fever.

"I related the whole adventure to them... so that they found the two pieces of the Queen's letter.

"Doubtless the unfortunate lady and gentleman, not daring to keep the occurrence secret, wrote all to the Queen, and sent back to her the torn letter."

Soon afterward, I was arrested and moved to the Bastille...

...and my two attendants disappeared.

What became of them?

They are dead.

Poisoned.

My enemy must have been very cruel, or hard beset by necessity, to assassinate these two innocent people.

In your family, monseigneur... necessity is stern.

Listen...and, in a few words, I will tell what has passed in France since the probable time of your birth.

The late King, Henry XIII, was long anxious about having an heir...

And on the 5th of September, 1638, his Queen, Anne of Austria, gave birth...

"...to a son.

"You are about to hear an account which few could now give...for it refers to a secret thought buried with the dead and entombed in the abyss of the confessional.

"The Queen lay in her room attended by her midwife...

"...whose name was Dame Perronnette...

"...soon, near at hand, the King showed the new-born to the nobility...

"Suddenly, unbeknownst to them, the Queen was again taken ill...

"...and the midwife quietly returned to her.

"...and all rejoiced.

"Soon, Dame Perronnette whispered to the King what had happened.

"He had a *second* son!

"The King's joy had turned to terror.

"As he and Mazarin knew, there is ground for doubting whether the twin who first makes his appearance is the elder by the laws of Heaven and nature.

"One day, the second son might dispute the first's claim to seniority...sowing discord...

"...and engendering *civil war!*

"That very night, the tutor and midwife spirited the second infant away in a carriage to a certain remote place...

"And today, only his mother remains alive to remember that he ever existed."

Monseigneur--in the house you inhabited for your first fifteen years, there were neither looking-glasses nor mirrors?

I have never heard those two words before.

Then--here is a portrait of King Louis XIV, who at this moment reigns upon the throne of France.

And here is a mirror.

It is the same face... except that the image I behold in the mirror has a mustache!

I think that I am lost! The King will never set me free.

But--which of the two is the King?

The one the miniature portrays-- or the glass reflects?

The King is he who is on the throne... who is not in prison...and who can cause others to be entombed here.

If you desire it, the King will be he who, quitting this dungeon, shall maintain himself upon the throne...upon which his friends shall place him.

I wish you to be King... for the good of humanity.

But-- what would then become of Louis?

If I restore you to your place on your brother's throne, he shall take yours in prison.

But I shall only do so...if you really want to be free...and to be King.

I...would be both.

Then I shall see you one more time only...on the day you leave these gloomy walls...

...my King.

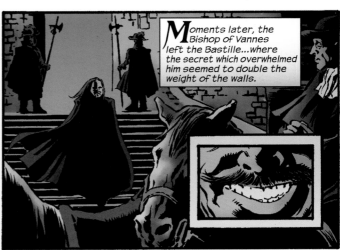

*M*oments later, the Bishop of Vannes left the Bastille...where the secret which overwhelmed him seemed to double the weight of the walls.

*T*he Bishop's carriage conveyed him to Vaux-le-Vicomte, the magnificent estate of M. Nicholas Fouquet, Surintendant--that is to say, primary tax collector--of all France.

*T*here, preparations were underway for a great fête which was to be held, in honor of Louis XIV...

*B*ut Aramis found Surintendant Fouquet in no very happy mood...

Why do you sigh, monseigneur?

The fête I suggested you give for the King is approaching.

And money is departing.

You promised me millions...

And you shall have them, the day after the King's entrée into Vaux.

My enemy, M. Colbert--the finance minister--poisons my sovereign's mind against me.

He is trying to convince Louis that I have stolen tax money to build this vast estate, which is greater than the King's.

Frankly, Bishop--I fear imprisonment!

Fear not...all will be well.

Meanwhile, I am back to Paris...when you shall have given me a certain letter of cachet.

A poor lad named Marchiali has been in the Bastille these ten years, for two Latin verses he made against the Jesuits.

And he has committed no other crime?

Beyond this, upon my honor, he is as innocent as you or I. So swears his poor, destitute mother.

Oh! Heaven! You sometimes bear with such injustice on earth--

--that I understand why there are wretches who doubt your existence.

The letter--and ten thousand francs for his mother.

Go! And I hope that God will bless those who are mindful of His poor!

So also do I hope.

That night, as Aramis once again dined with M. de Baisemeaux at the Bastille...

Monseigneur...

Eh? Oh, yes...the *courier* who had arrived.

You must wait till we have finished--

Oh, let us see what he has brought you, old friend...

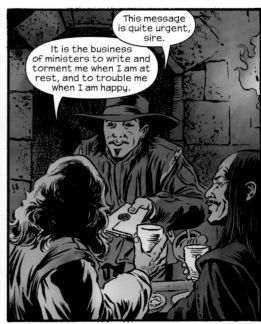

This message is quite urgent, sire.

It is the business of ministers to write and torment me when I am at rest, and to trouble me when I am happy.

An order of release! It is *"urgent"* to set free, this very night, a man who has been here ten years!

Well, we are at supper... and our affairs are urgent, too!

Dear Baisemeaux, I am a priest...and charity has higher claims upon me than hunger and thirst.

I entreat you, please release the poor devil at once.

Because *you* desire it...I shall summon my servant François.

François, tell the major to go and open the cell of M. Seldon, No. 3, Bertaudière.

"Seldon"? Surely you meant to say "Marchiali."

No...the letter said "Seldon," in large letters.

And I read "Marchiali" in even larger letters.

Yes--yes! Marchiali! 'Tis plainly written Marchiali!

The man of whom we have talked so much?

The very same prisoner whom, the other day...

...a priest, a confessor of our order, came to visit?

It is sometimes good, M. Baisemeaux, that the man of today should no longer know what the man of yesterday did.

But, to relieve your mind... I shall write a note approving the release of Marchiali.

Half an hour later, whilst Aramis watched from out of sight, Philippe was made acquainted with the order which set him at liberty...

You must swear never to reveal anything that you have seen or heard in the Bastille.

I swear with my lips on this crucifix.

Now you are free, monsieur...whither do you intend going?

I--I do not--

I am here to render the gentleman whatever service he may please to ask.

God have you in his holy keeping!

Good night to you, M. Baisemeaux.

As the carriage rattled over the pavement of the courtyard, Baisemeaux rejoiced that he held the letter of cachet...and the Bishop's personal note.

If any questioned his actions this night, they would prove that he did only that which was commanded of him by his superiors.

After tomorrow, you will sit upon the throne, from which the will of Heaven will have hurled your brother, without hope of return.

His blood will not be shed?

You will be sole arbiter of his fate.

I cannot take my brother's wife.

I will persuade Spain to consent to a divorce.

The imprisoned King will speak!

Aye--to the walls!

Monseigneur--I offer you a secluded estate, where you may let the years of your life roll away, if you have not the heart for our enterprise.

The choice is yours.

Before I determine, let me walk...and consult that still voice within me.

Driver! Halt the carriage!

Ten minutes is all I ask... and then you shall have your answer.

The ineffable whisper of liberty spoke to the Prince in so seducing a language that he could not restrain his emotion...and breathed a sigh of joy.

He inhaled the perfumed air...

...as it was wafted in gentle gusts across his uplifted face.

Then he returned to the carriage... and to Aramis.

Let us go where the crown of France is to be found!

You have perused all the notes I sent, to acquaint you with those who compose your court?

I know them by heart.

My mother, Anne of Austria, and all her sorrows.

Colbert, the minister of finance...

Your friend d'Artagnan... captain of the Musketeers.

The Comte de la Fère... the former Athos...

...and M. du Vallon... Porthos.

And what do you wish for yourself, Bishop?

Merely to be made, in due time, a Cardinal, monseigneur.

And, in due time, as I have given you the throne of France...

..you will confer on me the throne of St. Peter.

With what we may do together, not even Charlemagne will be able to reach to half your stature.

When you shall point out to me the necessary steps to be taken to secure your election as Pope...

...I will take them.

And they resumed their places in the carriage...

...which sped rapidly along the road leading to Vaux-le-Vicomte.

NEXT: HIGH TREASON